JABUTÍ
THE TORTOISE

A TRICKSTER TALE FROM THE AMAZON

TOLD AND ILLUSTRATED BY

Gerald McDermott

Harcourt, Inc.

San Diego   New York   London

Requests for permission to make copies of any part of the work
should be mailed to the following address: Permissions Department,
Harcourt, Inc., 6277 Sea Harbor Drive, Orlando, Florida 32887-6777.

www.harcourt.com

Library of Congress Cataloging-in-Publication Data
McDermott, Gerald.
Jabuti the tortoise: a trickster tale from the Amazon/told and illustrated
by Gerald McDermott.
p.   cm.
Summary: All the birds enjoy the songlike flute music of Jabuti, the tortoise,
except Vulture, who, jealous because he cannot sing, tricks Jabuti into riding
his back toward a festival planned by the King of Heaven.
1. Indians of South America—Amazon River Region—Folklore.
2. Tales—Amazon River Region. 3. Turtles—Folklore. [1. Indians of South
America—Amazon River Region—Folklore. 2. Folklore—Amazon River Region.
3. Turtles—Folklore. 4. Vultures—Folklore.] I. Title.
F2519.1.A6M33 2001
398.2′09811′0452792—dc21   00-11977
ISBN 0-15-200496-3

First edition
H G F E D C B A
Printed in Singapore

The illustrations in this book were done in gouache, colored pencil, and
colored ink on 300 lb. hot press Arches watercolor paper.
The display type and text type were set in Neue Neuland Light.
Color separations by Bright Arts Ltd., Hong Kong
Printed and bound by Tien Wah Press, Singapore
This book was printed on totally chlorine-free Nymolla Matte Art paper.
Production supervision by Sandra Grebenar and Ginger Boyer
Typography designed by Lydia D'moch

Jabuti (zha-boo-CHEE) is a central figure in the tribal lore
of the Amazon rain forest. Slow and short-legged, the little
tortoise is nevertheless portrayed as virtually invincible.
Through his cleverness, he is able to overcome larger, often
dim-witted foes. These mirthful trickster tales expose human
foibles and are enjoyed throughout Brazil.

The first collection of Jabuti stories, from the oral tradi-
tion of the Tupi-Guarani and other rain forest tribes, was
compiled by Charles Frederick Hartt and published in Rio de
Janeiro in 1875 under the title *Os Mitos Amazônicos da
Tartaruga*. Since then, the exploits of Jabuti have been retold
countless times.

Scholars believe some of the Jabuti stories, like the tales of
Brer Terrapin in the southern United States, have a common
origin in West Africa. Another cross-cultural link is the King
of Heaven, the great god Tupan, who appears throughout the
native mythology of the Americas as Thunderbird. The motif
of the turtle tumbling from the sky is found in many different
traditions, with examples as venerable as Aesop's "The Tortoise
and the Eagle," and "The Turtle and the Geese" from the
Panchatantra of ancient India.

In the present story, even though Jabuti's world is turned
upside down, a universal trickster theme prevails: Creation
comes from chaos.

—G. M.

Visit www.geraldmcdermott.com

For Tomás and Sofia

Jabuti the tortoise played a song on his flute.
His shell was smooth and shiny, and his song was sweet.

His music wove through the tangled vines
and floated above the treetops. All the
creatures of the rain forest listened to his song.

For some, Jabutí's song was sour.

Jaguar could remember when Jabutí tricked him into chasing his own tail.

Lizard could remember when Jabutí
tricked him into giving Jabutí a ride on his back.

Tapir could remember when Jabutí tricked him into a tug-of-war with Whale.

But the birds of the air loved Jabutí's music,
and they sang when he played.

All except Vulture, who could not sing at all.
He was jealous of Jabutí and waited for the
day when he could eat the little tortoise.

There came a time when all the birds of the air
were invited to a festival in heaven. The King
of Heaven called them together to sing, to rejoice,
and to receive his blessing.

When Jabutí saw the great gathering
of the birds, he wanted to go, too.

"I want to play my flute for the King of Heaven," he said.
Vulture laughed at him.

"I may not be able to make music like you," said Vulture,
"but I can spread my wings and soar all the way to heaven."

"Take me with you," Jabutí pleaded.

Vulture saw his chance.

"Climb on my back, little friend," he said.

Vulture spread his dark wings and rose up in the air. Jabutí held tight to Vulture's feathers as they flew high above the treetops. The dense forest and the great river stretched far below.

They had almost reached heaven when Vulture
suddenly swooped and turned upside down.

Jabutí lost hold of Vulture's feathers
and slipped off his back.

Jabutí went tumbling down through the sky.

The earth came rushing toward him, and he cried out:

> "Twigs and bushes,
> Flowers and trees,
> Move aside,
> Make way for me!"

All the plants and trees of the forest spread apart
to make way for Jabutí. But he had forgotten to
call to the rock. Jabutí came down on it with a *crack!*
and his smooth, shiny shell broke into pieces.

At that moment, the music of the festival in heaven stopped. The King of Heaven looked down and saw Vulture joining the other birds.

"Where is Jabuti?" asked the King of Heaven.

Vulture shrugged. "How would I know?" he answered.

"Jabutí wanted to play for me, and you offered to bring him here," said the King of Heaven sternly. "Tell me where he is!"

Vulture turned away from the King of Heaven and hid his head beneath his wing.

The King of Heaven commanded the birds
to search for Jabutí.

The birds filled the sky, flying high over the treetops,
swooping low through the tangled vines,
looking for the little tortoise.

Toucan, Macaw, and Hummingbird found Jabutí.
He was lying helplessly in the forest. His beautiful
shell was broken.

The birds gathered the pieces
and patched him together.

When they were done, Jabutí played a song of thanks for them.

And where the birds had touched Jabutí, they each took on a new color. Toucan got a red and yellow beak, Macaw, bright orange feathers, and Hummingbird, an emerald green belly.

Vulture stayed the same dull color. He still can't sing.

Jabutí the tortoise plays on his flute.
His music weaves through the tangled vines
and floats above the treetops.

His shell may be cracked and patched,
but his song is sweet . . .

at least to some.